Jen Hadfield lives in Shetland. Her first
Almanacs, won an Eric Gregory Award in 2003.
Her second collection, *Nigh-No-Place*, won the
T. S. Eliot Prize and was shortlisted for the Forward
Prize for Best Collection. She won the Edwin Morgan
Poetry Competition in 2012.

Also by Jen Hadfield in Picador

Byssus

Jen Hadfield

The Stone Age

PICADOR

First published 2021 by Picador
an imprint of Pan Macmillan
The Smithson, 6 Briset Street, London EC1M 5NR
EU representative: Macmillan Publishers Ireland Limited,
Mallard Lodge, Lansdowne Village, Dublin 4
Associated companies throughout the world
www.panmacmillan.com

ISBN 978-1-5290-3734-0

9 8 7 6 5 4 3 2 1

A CIP catalogue record for this book is available from the British Library.

Printed and bound by CPI Group (UK) Ltd, Croydon, CR0 4YY

Visit **www.picador.com** to read more about all our books
and to buy them. You will also find features, author interviews and
news of any author events, and you can sign up for e-newsletters
so that you're always first to hear about our new releases.

for my family

Contents

The Stone Age

0

0

0

0

0

0

0

0

0

Rockpool

Above the rockpool
everything is tilt or

rough, glazed in
weed like afterbirth

the sharp rocks
starry as the

domes of Istanbul
seedling barnacles

streaming down
the gutters of

the mosques
of the limpets

like falling stars.
This is no place

to show up
without a shell

all that protects us
from the press

of heaven –

Hardanger Fiddle & Nyckelharpa

So help me – I would rather write a song,
a wordless song for the
strings of the North –

Hardanger fiddle and

Nyckelharpa –
like jewels hewn in flaxen wood,
keys a delicate overbite.

Elfish devices in mother-of-pearl like
nights the sea calms
paler than the sky – short bow light

enough to touch the nerves of the North

fretful in a shiver
of sympathetic strings

feeling in their flat chests
how close the night has moored to   silence. Bored

wind gowling in the bars of the
gate, purr of surge when the night
is still, so help me – write

a song of unsettling
grace, perhaps an old folk-dance
in a weird time-signature,

a gawky
waltz, a
lonely march: gone off at a tangent,

popped back to say   *it was just*

a random thought –

an interrupted cadence –
a whistle under the breath –

Granny whose gaze

Granny whose gaze
was very much the moon
half-full is in her green
coat in the holly wood.

Granny whose gaze was
very much the moon
half-full is not far off,
second rung of the

the stepladder up
in the boughs of the
baking apple tree.
Her gaze dwindling

through its last quarter,
Granny declared with
unusual apology *I don't
like to see the new moon*

*through glass at least
I tend to think it's
unlucky for me*, turning
from her reflection

in her clear dusk cardigan –
because she couldn't abide
to be idle, and so prized
the days she got a lot

done

Dolmen

Standing stone, let's
talk about
You! Who knows
how deep this grief goes
down – in your thick waist
and whalebone skirt –
       goodnessknows
how deep and wide –
twinkling modestly with
garnet, feldspar –

whiffing
(faintly) of bruised
mushroom.

Now, we learnt in
school about Deep
Time. Six

o'clock shadow: lichen.
Pouringdownlikeporridge:
lichen. But humankind
are brief, soft

fireworks, prone
to go off at a moment's
notice. Are we even speaking the
same language? Urgently

we hammer at your
boarded-up window,
        rattle and try

your grittygrey door!

(Because my sentence is
lava slow and
sometimes mangled
conglomerate
grey lag of language a
wingbeat behind

words come halt

and misonym
but your intervention
was unnecessary
in fact I simply
turned away to
gawp out through

my Northern pane

thought's a
fog dark sea
green lens
glittering with a
thousand facets)

Gaelic

It's not ok to rub your head against air like a cat. It's not
ok to be too sincere. I know you can tell I'm cribbing
as I go, and when I ask, 'What would you say is *your*
mother tongue?' I'm the last surviving speaker
of my language. But when I'm fully exhausted of
conjugating feeling, parsing silence between speaker
and listener, and remembering to ask
questions, direct but not too
direct, and pausing to really hear the answer,
and hearing you, really hearing you, but under
the ribs, sensing slack
water . . . it does sometimes happen
I let an oar drop.
I know how it looks.
And I see your shock.
Like you saw a face through a dark river.
To you I'm suddenly speaking Gaelic,
like language translated
into slow light –
and swift dark –

(The foundation of this drystane dael

is where my head is at

indomitable lump like a troll's

boulder   bluntened bubble   a

mere ten tonnes

 Shoved into the
front line amongst
a dapper infantry
here's my cranium

unfashionably

sincere   here's your small

talk tesselate quick stable splintery

a wall made of common currency
moss-draped something
like a veil   a hundred mile
of complacent coherent competent
drystone   cohesive
cognitivecognisant
stone   then this greenish lode
creased smilingly   waxy
as ambergris it doesn't
go   like a naked elbow
in a bunch of flowers)

Pictish Stone

I lay my hands on this basking thing
(since you don't wake when nurses turn you) –
in the year's first warmth, do I feel it
stir? We watch and wonder how earth-fast

you are, surfacing from more than sleep –
tickled, when you wake, if you wake at
all, to find us all sitting here, on
our skiing holiday up Grouse

Mountain! You say *gin, yes!* and gaily, *I
just feel reborn!* then slip away too
fast to drink it, and soon you'll keep to
yourself entirely, retracting

a million, sparkling tentacles.
Here's a riddle – who's more deeply
private than a stone, tucked up inside a
twinkling rind: dreams – of the man-bird,

the bear and boar – written all over
their face? Our job is not to wait, but
to watch – so you can creep out right
from under our noses – like a

child who is just learning how to hide –

Midwife

All night, Meg
looks after newborns.

Her shift is full of First This and First
That.

Corkscrewing into her pupil's soil,
a child's first gaze takes thistly root.

She hurries him
to his drugged mother.

Meg creeps in at eight and
then the flat
is ward-quiet. Quiet –

     floorboards squealing
and latches that click like toes, the
little groan of the kitchen door,
and high above the range of
human hearing,

damp pants
on the pulley, pleepsing

like bats. So Meg is awake again in no time at all,
bearing her ribcage high like a lantern

(and a moth flitters round it, the
colour of fur) –

(skimming over floorboards like
a person who's

learnt to walk on fire) –

Ert-fast

I midwife a hundred
rocks in a day: red
rocks, glistening
like anvils.

Each
must be delivered
in its own way, uncleaving
root-veined fascias –

with shocking noise they
broach the light – red-
cheeked and muddy, marred
and birth-marked,
leaving in sucking soil

the imprint of their
darling faces.

I prise the sticking
children, backbreaking work –
but no poor me, although

I've been a missionary
while you raised your
one or two –

I have this
consolation of
strong and silent types,

my hundred
quiet ones,

that take to talking
late and slow —

(See how the leopard
slug in controlled free

fall

bumps
its eyes against
the sharpness of my lichens
see the thumbprint from
the day it was made
see its strong cetacean

tail   the world is always
hurrying me along the headrush
heavens dirl round my anchor I
see your lives flare

                        and softly fall

but while you press me for my
answer

        I'm still considering
your first question)

Umbrella

Thirty years ago, as this poem began, I thought people speaking another language were like people talking under umbrellas. Now wardens are out clearing the flood-traps, and gutter and hill run like a river, in little surges like rills of clear pleasure; and drops pop the fabric between the vanes, as if all I can throw up between me and the rain is the bivouac of my own eardrum.

On the threshold of the caff, I fold the umbrella to a long, dripping dart. The customers keep tracking in rain, splashing like sparrows in talk and clatter. Three women: three wells of standing water. One saying very calmly, 'one minute you're laughing, the next you're bawling your eyes out.' And another, 'but life has to go on, doesn't it?'

I open your book, to weather the present storm in its shelter. From time to time, no urgency whatsoever, a woman mops the slick from the floor. Now I see I'm the one under the umbrella, and everyone else is standing in the rain: gilled, they swim through its drenching blether and never look like they're drowning –

(You said what you said –
and I turned to stone   it's
too easy for this to happen
grieving in the pasture in my smock
of sorrel red clover bog
asphodel   fog pouring over
the whalebacked hill
fog and flowers a thousand years
the rustle of the fog the
soft roar of the pouring fog)

Gyö

You tell me people like me don't have feelings. And you
wonder why I don't call myself a person. I say rage is a cold
cliff; longing, a skerry. Pleasure is a kelp-hung arch, glittered
constantly by the licking of the wave. Tenderness is a
sandbar. Joy an overhang of shiversome schist. You navigate
the arch, the skerry; you land, cast off; you take a pleasure
cruise; a stripped feather twirls on the oily swell, the sea-
stack recedes into heavy, bright mist. But I'm the quartz, the
basalt, the gabbro. And if I had children like people have
children, I would creche them in a daisied gentleness, they'd
fledge from the gargling kindergarten of the gyö —

Oyea

It always seems like you shout
your feelings like a town crier,
and I proclaim my feelings like
a town crier, and folk don't so

much share as ring out their
feelings like crowds of town
criers, turning this way and
that, throwing their chins to

the sky to toll with a strong
downward clang the feelings:
summons we perpetually serve
on each other. As if at the edict

of some abdicating king, perhaps
a stark-bollock-naked one, his
lieutenant standing nude in the
king's name too, Armistice

and christening, the alarum
peal: I feel! I feel! I feel! I feel!

Skunk Cabbage

I have no idea where I comes
to an end. Perhaps in walls I frantically throw
up, hands flachtering like birds between
the stones   or in skin touchy as an
electric fence   and when you
cross this moat of oily water,
to plant your foot on the
welcome mat of my
liver, I burp
out the naked truth
like a novelty doorbell, or
something spouting from

a vegetal gland: a
rattlesnake
pistil, waxy-white,

sheathed
in a fountain
of indigenous
leaves —

Need Ice Wealth Hail

'The razor clam has a long and powerful "foot" which enables
it to make its way through wet sand like a knife through
butter, dodging danger by a swift descent downwards.'

North Atlantic Seafood Cookery, Alan Davidson

How should
you pray to
a buried god?
Like this —

on your knees
in the ebb,
wrist buried in
sliding sand

, seized by
something like
a bolt of
lightning. Holding

fast the struggling
being still
throwing its
shapes through

the winter
gale: the broad
fingernail of
a buried giant

become the
inward pull of
come become
prayer – like a

mandrake –
yelps
of white
noise. And flung

up and out of the
waves together,
the bleeding
supplicant

and the long,
dripping shell:
blurting white
runes we can

almost
decipher –

Nied!

Is!

Feoh!

Haegl! −

Cliff

I say, there's no such thing as the Edge. You
say, *So whaddayoucall this?,*
prancing along it to make   your point. A
hungover six-pack in a   greasy,
gold bearskin? A herniate,
black, basaltic rainbow? After the
rain,   the cracks
are showing. Bits
fall off – it happens all the time. It's   as if this
whole time I've been dreaming, snoozing
in its floating meadow
, blowholes
booming in bowel and womb,
while this hang and fly and
stretch and cramp, this
sweetly-reeking
inside-out cathedral, has been
trembling on its marks,
waiting on the day it calves
to fizz into the
sea in sparkle!

I say, that kind
of thinking is
unsafe —

     just think of
the sound as it
slid into the
sea —

like the
love leaving your

lover's
face —

Nudibranch

I ease my naked body down
into the rockpool's closet, clinging
to the vertical rocks with my soles,
hanging a moment
before I let myself fall   slowly
as a dim slip that shrugs off
its hanger in a deep, green changing room,
air shouting silently from my struck
lungs, I would try on
the old clothes to
see if they still fit. Dropping
to the velveted floor the seizing
onesie of brillo hair, the sweat-sheath
that horripilates with urchinous
buttons – each breaking wave
dousing me of costume,
comfortably
divested of my name.

Perhaps still some permeable
notion of self –

arabesques
of albumen –

prongs subliming
to tender flame

condensing
down to antlers

and weed and warm and
warm and

weed –

Limpet

Stop, now you're
home, and consider
what that feels like –
don't stop, continue

to whirl, an introvert
tornado, across the
flooded rockpool
in an ease of gypsy

skirts – cyclonic,
high and wet. This
is not a thing
to sit tight upon –

locked to your home-
scar against the
migraine of the waves –
this rebate will wait

that you can spin home to
like cup to saucer –
matching every chip
in your shell to its

own rocky rostrum.
Clamp down –
turn the key of
yourself in the lock

of yourself, fasten –
with a hundred
infinitesimal
mortices –

Rhubarb

In winter, low
tide comes to the rhubarb
box and bares
stiff reefs of coral

, midsummer – we rustle rhubarb, lean
and feral, from its driftwood corral. It's
late

      but I'm not tired at all, as you
yearn over the rotting fence – I say
  Careful! You'll be
man overboard! then you plunge like a

pearl-fisher into creaking billows,
  clipping thin petioles with
your special knife

. In the west, the sky is pink as rhubarb. You say
you're not that into
sunsets.

We hike to the far cliffs
as if the night will never fall, my
bouquet of rhubarb

weirdly heavy, like
an armful of water . . . millefiore. I say,

They called him the Rhubarb Rustler. You say
everything's early this year.

You say, the rain is good when it's soft.
You say, it's fine
to have children to borrow

. Now

a bird begins
to whistle. The rusty ears creak
and swivel. Dim green of the

hill is yawning
visible and the little-voiced
dawn will soon be audible – and

   did I say how late it is? In
the East, the sky is pink as rhubarb. So

we trim, at both ends, these
lean, sour, freckled stems,
and I say

   I'm just
         so tired —

Ben Wyvis

Would you tell me
the whole thing again,
from the top, now
the long, wide strath is

made simple with snow,
each word minted, a
quiet impression,
a trail of glazed

footprints, long after
the thaw. Walk me
through it again? – Now
I can hear a little more –

now the memory's calm,
monumental in snow
– I track the spoor
of your wicking words,

you long gone, the
wound of your trail
thin floes of clear gore –
I cradle in my palm

each floating question –

to be honest with you —

to be quite frank —

I have to admit —

I must say —

In all honesty —

to be

perfectly

honest

Drimmie

When I finally ask about the Revolution, your voice changes.
Up to now, you've been courtly, thoughtful: your graciousness
is careful and comprehensive. It's been hard to know if we
understand each other – shades of me speaking like you,
shades of you speaking like me. I think you liked the Spittal
of Glenshee: fog-lights on just for a moment as the road
climbed the mountain, off again as it dropped downhill. In
Cairo, you say, one can miss the sunset. Here, It Going Dark
has taken an hour. I wonder what Drimmie might mean . . .
a fleeting moment in the quality of dusk, precise to a degree.
In small, ebbing towns, men stand in awe of the spectacle of
your driving. You aim for the brake-lights and then swerve
out. How can we say when the day is done? I'm afraid I still
have more questions, and not just because I hope to keep
you talking, a trick I would like to play on you, until the sun
is definitely down – even if I must see you turned to stone –

Snowline

Hare, your sprinter's legs are too long
for the valley.

You've been outrunning
rabbits, cramming
rabbit manners, trying
to fit in!

Your head
is a thimble.

Honest, immaterial;
like a rabbit but with long, gold
eyes – it looks like something's wrong
with you.

Then an idea comes like a fright,
silvering your fur!

Flushed grouse
are ideas, ravens
flying upside-
down

are ideas!

Loup the border that can take
you home.

Blowing so white
you burn with a blue
flame.

Running like water
until you run clear –

Shadow

So this is where I left my
shadow – italic,
underweight – stashed
like a tushkar in the

corner of your kitchen.
What in god's name have
you been feeding it?
Dark plates of hashed

hellery, like pie for birds;
long winter of the berried
dark – I can't believe my
delinquent shadow – fat

and glossy – full as a tick –
muddy shadow running amok –
shagging this bright rock –
the hill – snaps mockingly to

attention when I cry
Heel! Welling bottomless
at my foot – roosts in my
clavicle – opens its throat.

You press on me the leash
of my shadow. Say, *Open*
the granite wardrobe of your breast.
Fold in your shadow

like a warm, winter coat –

(Fear opens a cave in your
brain   I colour it in with intimate
crystals   the problem is the
yoyoing Beyond   your
hill-buddy vanishing in three

swift

strides

a baleen sweep of yellow rain

an amputated shout   !   o

won't you live forever in
your mountain's pocket? But
you wobble downhill hand

in   shoot the bolt
                        of the hill-
hand   gate

leave your
footprints in
my wet meadow)

Strimmer

Strimmer, you butcher,
you-as-soul are the hardest to
imagine. A poor soul, a kind soul, a
good soul – easy! – soul a deep
ladle, soul a ladder. How
intimately we tangle with our
tools – grafting them into
our brains like prosthesis – I'm
appalled by your skinny neck,
thrusting the flat howl of your face
into the meadow's tangle,
screaming at stinging nettle, couch-
grass, clover; sending flying
little moth-scrap-souls.
I can't find a thing to
admire in you –
thrash-metal strap-on whose
obsession with yield makes
yielding impossible –
    stumbling
onward in evangelical
fury, roaring
your hateful rhetoric. All small
voices drowned out in the carnage, the fresh
green blood
flying in my face –

Mortis and Tenon

As soon as I decided to build a gate,
the locked landscape uttered
gates: gates I'd never noticed

before. Gates grew, fast as bamboo:
a yellow portcullis, spruce with
yolk-thick paint; the flexible

hill-gate: a curlew's wing.
Two stout strainers at Gössigarth
promised to sproot a gate, come

Spring. I begged chisels,
several kinds of saws. I asked
which way the brace should

run, to bear the burden of the
hanging wing –
on their notional hinges, gates,

unborn, ached – until
it was known
as Gate-gate, and mine

the most debated gate
in the isle. I practised
then fitted the difficult joint.

A second coat dried.

Oval knots blinked open the paint.

What else might we dream,
before the godly eyes
of gates, as mortis knits to tenon

with a tap, and gate after gate after
gate sweeps wide its
slow and drooping wing? –

Nettles

You tell me *the hope is the worst*, and
I say yes, like nettles, the way they
seize hold of the soil's dark meat.
Out at midnight with the garden fork,

I mean to eradicate hope, like an
amputation of the nervous system,
I will parse its searing sea-ferns clear
of my body. But as I haul on this

red-hot rope, what I hear is the
last-chance clanking of a drawbridge,
and as I drag this scalding root,
each and every snapped-off

shoot spouts its manyheads of
hope,

      and (to misquote)

many waters   cannot
quench hope –

Neverspel

Unfurling a washed-up scroll of birch-bark —
thick hangnail from a Canadian tree —
to re-read the history of the day we found

it — having rolled and unrolled this creaking
codex — gingerly squeezing to test its dry ache —
to nuzzle and snuffle its dusty sweetness—

I'll have to chuck back this betulant boat: after all this time,
all it does is bark back to the forest —

all it can think about is the forest —

Scythe

Considering my wild yard,
you recommend a scythe –
except in your tongue
it sounded like *scye.*

It sounded like you said a sigh –
in the Northern countries,
to say yes is a sigh – a
kind of swift, indrawn gasp –

like the trick of swallowing
a knife. Times past, folk worked . . . *fok wrought*
wi a scye . . . met hairst
with a scythe, a kind of

acquiescence – the keen edge
put on summer; summer
tilted to the winter
good. It swees like a papercut –

the land regrets its violet
hood. It's only one way to
keep up with time, one beat
behind each brief, hushed smile

subtracting from the sward
with the singing
scythe   I step I sigh I
step I *scye* –

Wheelbarrow

You gimme me a hurl in the old
iron wheelbarrow. Then
I give you a
hurl, and at the cattle-grid cowp
you out, an awkward load of
tailings and ore, and we laugh with stiff,
out-of-practice faces. It's midsummer,
midnight –
everything's possible. The barrow's an
ox, sinking down on its knees;
before the alphabet, there is
this barrow – a folded sheet of iron, two
pipes – runs on a self-soothing,
whimpering
wheel. *Goodnight*
goats and sleeptight Ciderhouse,
goodnight Leslie and da Lass, it
picks up speed with a sad, goldrush
whistle, skimming like an ancient
ray – coughs rust and warbles –
now the long brae, complaining
uncomplainingly, like cattle
slipped from their winter byres –
beginning to
hasten and leap just
a little. Singing *useful*

work versus
useless toil –

here comes a
heyday of deep,
black soil –

Strom

When you suddenly have a
teenager, pale as bone,
leading on smolts with
his quiet, persuasive hook –

even I have to wonder where
time has gone. Slow
and silent because it's been so long,
content to root down into bog and

blugga, I like to tell myself
people need stone – maybe I
can be your earthly anchor. Our
wine-glasses are big as goldfish

bowls . . . we set them on fence-posts
to cross the barbed wire, stow them
empty in your deep coat-
pockets, stems clinking

against stones
and bones, as if grimy ballast
from bog and shore could stop us
all from spinning

away. But the tide's
coming in, sweetheart, nice
and slow, star-trails invisible
hula around us, and peerie troots

make impressive splashes;
his fingerprints tarnish
their vital slime as he twists the
hooks in their cheeks in dismay –

Don'tdothis, don'tdothisto
        me – I'msorry!
flinging them
into their freedom

        lea

                p! –

(Your tongue was fastforwarded
mine is a doglick a
treacly dopplering
you know I like   (I liked)   you very
much (like you love
hummingbirds)

how I love(d)
your consciousness   its
strobing blur)

Radiant Star

And at night we never pulled the curtains –
what do you think curtains are for
except to frame all this nothing-to-hide? –

hameaboots, a sun-bright moon empties itself
over roofs and ruins: you can still see
the poor old body inby –

and if you go along her, it'll be *my son
was a fisherman, my man was a fisherman*, and so
on right back to the house she was born in –

and between the heavens and
da Foula Haaf, floodlights
of the Radiant Star –

(Sound travels so far on the quiet evenings especially in mis

the human cough of sheep   the graveyard gate
with its quiet hinge

                                                        and swans

                              on a still day
you hear the beat of their wings
something like the creaking of oars

a longboat rowed from the sky's shore
the hoarse cry of the oarsmen

Notes & Acknowledgements

ert-fast (Shetland) – like bedrock, a stone solidly fixed in
   earth
gyö (Shetland) – steep-sided inlet
pleepse – to cry, as a bird; by extension to humans, to whine
flachterin (Shetland) – fluttering
'How should you pray to a buried god?', poem, John Glenday
'Useless work versus useless toil' – William Morris
neverspel, also called *Willy-lowes, Willy White's Candle* and
   Willy Buck's Candle (Shetland) – a roll of birch bark
   washed up by the tide
blugga (Shetland) – marsh-marigold
peerie (Shetland) – little
tushkar (Shetland) – a peat spade
swees (Shetland) – stings

Thanks to the publishers of the following anthologies,
pamphlets, radio programmes and magazines in which some
of these poems have appeared:

The Rialto (90); *Poetry Review* (Vol. 107, No. 4 & Vol. 106,
No. 4); *Mortis & Tenon*, Little Windows Press, (2018);
The Shelter Stone, The Artist and the Mountain, ed. John
Glenday and Eddie Summerton, The Strict Nature Reserve,
and The Mountain Bothies Association (2017); *Conversations
on a Bench*, Overtone Productions (2019)

Thank you to Cove Park, The Causley Trust and Moniack Mhor for residencies in 2018 and 2019, where some of these poems were written.

Thank you Don, for encouraging me to run with it, and to Lindsay Nash and Rachel Smyth for their patience and precision when it came to typesetting.

I'm grateful to Creative Scotland, who awarded Lottery Funding to support the writing of *The Stone Age* and to give a series of public workshops and readings exploring neurodiversity.